Babies don't walk they ride!

A BRUBAKER, FORD & FRIENDS BOOK,
an imprint of The Templar Company Limited

First published in the UK
in 2015 by by Templar Publishing,
an imprint of The Templar Company Limited,
Deepdene Lodge, Deepdene Avenue, Dorking, Surrey, RH5 4AT, UK
www.templarco.co.uk

First edition

ISBN 978-1-78370-141-4 (Hardback)
ISBN 978-1-78370-186-5 (Softback)

Printed in China

B|F|&|F

BRUBAKER, FORD & FRIENDS

AN IMPRINT OF THE TEMPLAR COMPANY LIMITED

Babies
don't walk
they ride!
Kathy Henderson
Lauren Tobia
N S

Babies don't walk...

...they ride!

B
A

Babies don't run...they glide!

Strolling in buggies
and back-packs and slings,

Rolling in trolleys...

and car seats and things,

Bumping around
all over the place...

with a scowl or a howl
or a smile on their face,

A
B

Charging along
like charioteers,

Flying down hills,
and up in the air,

Huggled and cuddled and carried along,

if babies could talk they'd be singing this song...

Babies don't walk

they ride!

GOODNIGHT